ABIGAIL SPELLS

CROWN

EGG

FLY

HOUSE

BY **ANNA ALTER**

Alfred A. Knopf

New York

For Grace

THIS IS A BORZOI BOOK PUBLISHED BY ALFRED A. KNOPF

Copyright © 2009 by Anna Alter

Published in the United States by Alfred A. Knopf, an imprint of Random House Children's Books,
a division of Random House, Inc., New York.

Knopf, Borzoi Books, and the colophon are registered trademarks of Random House, Inc.

Visit us on the Web! www.randomhouse.com/kids

Educators and librarians, for a variety of teaching tools, visit us at www.randomhouse.com/teachers

Library of Congress Cataloging-in-Publication Data
Alter, Anna
Abigail spells / by Anna Alter. — 1st ed.
p.   cm.
Summary: George helps his best friend Abigail practice for the city spelling bee, then cheers her up when she makes a mistake.
ISBN 978-0-375-85617-4 (trade) — ISBN 978-0-375-95617-1 (lib. bdg.)
[1. Best friends—Fiction. 2. Friendship—Fiction. 3. Spelling bees—Fiction.] I. Title.
PZ7.A4635Abi 2009
[E]—dc22
2008024529

The illustrations in this book were created using acrylic paint.

MANUFACTURED IN CHINA
April 2009
10 9 8 7 6 5 4 3 2 1
First Edition

Abigail and George did everything together.

Abigail danced the cha-cha
while George played
the maracas.

C-H-A C-H-A C-H-A

Abigail struck a pose
while George painted
her portrait.

Abigail always had interesting
stories to tell, and George
loved to listen to them.

Once upon a T-I-M-E . . .

But there was one thing Abigail liked to do better than anything else. More than anything, Abigail loved to spell.

She spelled in the morning while she brushed her teeth.

B-R-U-S-H B-R-U-S-H

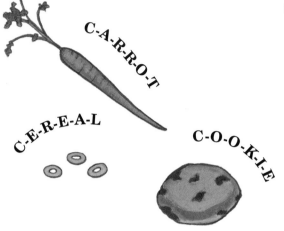

C-A-R-R-O-T

C-E-R-E-A-L

C-O-O-K-I-E

She spelled during lunch when she opened her lunch box.

And she spelled at night before going to sleep.

Sleep tight, Abigail!

Good N-I-G-H-T, George!

Then one day, Abigail saw something that made her jump up and down. In the hallway at school was a sign that read *Spelling Bee Next Friday. Winners will spell at the City Fair!* She could barely contain her excitement.

"I'll help you practice!" said George. "How do you spell 'apple'?"

"A-P-P-L-E!" cried Abigail.

"How about 'book'?" asked George.

"B-O-O-K!"

"What about 'clock'?"

"C-L-O-C-K!"

Abigail could spell just about everything.

Finally, the day of the spelling bee arrived. First came math. Abigail raised her hand to answer the question on the board.

"T-E-N!" she said proudly.

Then came music. Mr. Potter brought out a box with some letters on it. George looked at Abigail. She raised her hand and smiled.

"B-E-L-L-S!" said Abigail.

Next Mr. Potter asked everyone to return to their desks. Abigail looked around the room. She opened and closed her notebook. Then she opened it again. Abigail was ready.

A bell rang and it was time for the spelling bee.

"Wish me L-U-C-K!" she shouted.

Abigail raced to the auditorium. Her heart pounded as she made her way across the stage. She couldn't wait to begin.

George found a seat in the
second row. The lights went
down and he held his breath.

Mr. Potter went row by row. He asked each of his students how to spell a word, then listened for the answer.

Sofia sat two seats away from Abigail. She spelled "S-H-I-P," then sat down again. Mr. Potter nodded.

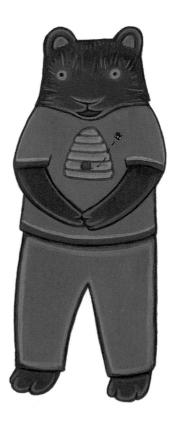

Then Benjamin spelled the word "banana," but he added an extra "n" and he was out.

Finally, it was Abigail's turn. She stood up.
She looked for George in the audience, but it was
too dark to see. Suddenly she felt hot.

"How do you spell 'elephant'?" asked Mr. Potter.

"E-L-E-" she began, but her mind went blank.
"F-" Her tummy felt funny.
"A-N-T," she said quickly.

Abigail sat down. She had made a mistake.

"I'm sorry," said Mr. Potter.

She would not spell in the City Fair Spelling Bee.

On the way home, Abigail did not spell anything. Even when George asked her if there was a "q" in the word "peanut."

The next day, George brought over his maracas. But Abigail didn't feel like dancing.

He pulled out his paintbrushes. But Abigail didn't want to be in a picture.

He asked her to tell him a story. But Abigail wouldn't utter a peep.

She just didn't know what to say.

George thought for a moment. "I have a story to tell you," he said finally. "Once upon a time there were a bear and a bird who did everything together."

Abigail looked up. She had never heard George tell a story before.

"Then one day, the bird stopped doing all the things she liked to do, and the bear was worried. He missed his friend. He thought she was a great dancer, made the perfect portrait, and was the best speller he'd ever met."

Abigail smiled. "That is a great story," she said. "But you forgot one important part. The bird was very glad that the bear was her F-R-I-E-N-D."

S-A-N-D T-W-I-G F-O-R-T R-O-C-K D-I-G T-R-U-C-K

George knew exactly what she meant.